The Tale of Old Mr. Crow

Arthur Scott Bailey

The Tale of Old Mr. Crow

I

THE OUTLAW

A good many of the forest-people claimed that old Mr. Crow was an outlaw. They said he was always roving about, robbing Farmer Green of his corn and his chickens, and digging up the potatoes when they shot their sprouts above the surface of the potato-patch. And everybody was aware that the old gentleman stole eggs from the nests of his smaller neighbors. It was even whispered that Mr. Crow had been known to devour baby robins.

But perhaps some of the things said of him were not true. Though if he really was an outlaw he seemed to enjoy being one. He usually laughed whenever Johnnie Green or his father tried to catch him, or when they attempted to frighten him. And on the whole he was quite the boldest, noisiest, and most impertinent of all the creatures that lived in Pleasant Valley.

His house stood in a tall elm, not too far from the cornfield. And those that dwelt near him never could complain that the neighborhood was quiet.... It was never quiet where old Mr. Crow was.

Many of the smaller birds feared him. But they couldn't help laughing at him sometimes—he was so droll, with his solemn face, his sedate walk, and his comical gestures. As for his voice, it was loud and harsh. And those that heard too much of it often wished that he would use it less.

Mr. Crow's best friends sometimes remarked that people did not understand him. They said that he helped Farmer Green more than he injured him, for he did a great deal in the way of eating beetles, cutworms and grasshoppers, as well as many other insects that tried to destroy Farmer Green's crops. So you see he had his good points, as well as his bad ones.

For a number of years Mr. Crow had spent each summer in Pleasant Valley, under the shadow of Blue Mountain. He usually arrived from the South in March and left in October. And though many of his friends stayed in the North and braved the winter's cold and storms, old Mr. Crow was too fond of a good meal to risk going hungry after the snow lay deep upon the ground. At that season, such of his neighbors as remained behind often dined upon dried berries, which they found clinging to the trees and bushes. But so long as Mr. Crow could go where it was warmer, and find sea food along the shore, he would not listen to his friends' pleas that he spend the winter with them.

"Until I can no longer travel 'as the crow flies,' I shall not spend a winter here," he would say to them with a solemn wink. That was one of his favorite jokes. He had heard that when anybody asked Farmer Green how far it was to the village he always answered, "It's nine miles as the crow flies" — meaning that it was nine miles in a straight line.

Old Mr. Crow thought that the saying was very funny. But then, he usually laughed at Farmer Green, no matter what he said or did.

You can see that Mr. Crow was no respecter of persons.

II

SOMETHING LOST

It may seem a strange thing for old Mr. Crow to have had no other name—such as John, or James, or Josephus. But that was the way he preferred it to be. Indeed, his parents had given him another name, years before. But Mr. Crow did not like it. And after he grew up he dropped the name. To tell the truth, the reason for his coming to Pleasant Valley, in the beginning, was because no one knew him there. And though his new friends thought it odd that he should be called simply "Mr. Crow," he was satisfied.

Of course, that was when he was younger. As the years passed he became known as "old Mr. Crow." But no one called him that except behind his back. And since he knew nothing of that, it never annoyed him in the least.

Now, Mr. Crow had spent a good many pleasant seasons in Pleasant Valley. And nobody had ever found out much about him. But at last there came a day when he was very much upset. He was roaming through the woods on a sunny afternoon when someone called to him.

He stopped. And presently a person in a bright blue coat came hurrying up. It was a noisy fellow known as Jasper Jay, who was new in the neighborhood.

"I thought I recognized you," he shouted to Mr. Crow. "As soon as I saw you fly past I said to myself, 'That looks like Cousin—'"

Mr. Crow stopped him just in time. It was true that the two were cousins.

One look at their big feet and their big bills would have told you that.

Now, Mr. Crow sometimes saw Jasper on the trips he made each fall and spring. And Jasper knew Mr. Crow's name. He had almost said it, too, at the top of his boisterous voice.

"What's the matter?" Jasper Jay inquired, for Mr. Crow was looking all around. "Have you lost anything?"

"Yes!" said Mr. Crow. "I've lost my name. And I don't want to find it again, either."

What he was really doing was this: He was peering about to see whether anybody might be listening.

Jasper Jay's mouth fell open—he was so astonished.

"Why, what do you mean, Cousin—"

Mr. Crow stopped him again.

"Don't call me that!" he said severely. "I'm known here as 'Mr. Crow.'

And I'll thank you to call me by that name and no other."

That astonished Jasper Jay all the more, because he had never known Mr.

Crow to thank anybody for anything.

"Well, well!" he murmured faintly. And then it was Mr. Crow's turn to be surprised, for he had never before heard his cousin Jasper speak in anything but the loudest scream.

Then Mr. Crow explained that he had never liked the name his parents had given him and that he wanted nobody in Pleasant Valley to learn what it was.

"You must promise me," said Mr. Crow—and there was a dangerous glitter in his eye—"you must promise me that you'll never speak my name again."

"Why, certainly!" Jasper Jay replied. "I'm glad to oblige you, I'm sure. And I promise that I'll never, never, never again mention your name aloud, Cousin Jim."

There! The secret is out! Jasper Jay said Mr. Crow's name without once thinking what he was about. And Mr. Crow was so angry that he gave his cousin a sound beating, on the spot.

"I'll teach you," he said, "to do as you're told!" And he did. For after that Jasper Jay always remembered that to him, as to everybody else, his big black cousin must be known only as "Mr. Crow."

You see, "Jim Crow" was a name that Mr. Crow could not abide. The mere
sound of it made him wince. And he was not a person of tender feelings,
either.

III

THE GIANT SCARECROW

Farmer Green always claimed that Mr. Crow was a ruffian and a robber.

"That old chap has been coming here every summer for years," he said to his son Johnnie one day. "I always know him when I see him, because he's the biggest of all the crows that steal my corn."

That was Farmer Green's way of looking at a certain matter. But old Mr. Crow regarded it otherwise. He knew well enough what Farmer Green thought

of his trick of digging up the newly planted corn. And his own idea and Farmer Green's did not agree at all.

Now, this matter was something that old Mr. Crow never mentioned unless somebody else spoke of it first. And then Mr. Crow would shake his head slowly, and sigh, and say:

"It's strange that Farmer Green doesn't understand how much I help him. I'm as busy as I can be all summer long, destroying insects that injure his crops. And since I help Farmer Green to raise his corn, I'm sure I have as good a right to a share of it as the horses that plough the field, or the men that hoe it. Farmer Green gives them corn to eat. But he never once thinks of giving me any."

You see, there are always two sides to every question. And that was Mr. Crow's. But Farmer Green never knew how Mr. Crow felt about the matter.

And every spring, at corn-planting time, he used to set up scarecrows

in his cornfield, hoping that they would frighten the crows away.

And so they did. At least, some of the younger crows were afraid of those straw-stuffed dummies, with their hats tipped over their faces, or upon one side, and their empty sleeves flapping in the winds that swept through the valley. But old Mr. Crow was too wise to be fooled so easily. He would scratch up the corn at the very feet of a scarecrow—and chuckle at the same time.

It must not be supposed that Farmer Green did not know what was going on. He often caught sight of Mr. Crow in the cornfield. But it always happened that Mr. Crow saw him too. And Farmer Green could never get near the old rogue.

At last Johnnie Green's father spent a whole evening trying to think of some way in which to outwit Mr. Crow. And by bedtime he had hit upon a plan that he liked.

The next day, with Johnnie to help him, he set to work to build a monster scarecrow. It was twice as high as the tallest man that was ever seen. And for a hat Farmer Green set on its straw head a huge tin pan, which glittered when the sun shone upon it.

"That'll fix him!" said Farmer Green, as he stood off and looked at the giant. And as for his son Johnnie, he danced up and down and shouted—he was so pleased.

But Mr. Crow was not pleased when he flew toward the cornfield the next day and saw the great figure of a man there, with a terrible glittering helmet upon his head. And Mr. Crow noticed something upon the giant's shoulder that looked very like a gun.

The old gentleman swerved quickly to one side and never stopped his flight until he had reached the woods.

And that night Farmer Green felt quite merry.

"I've scared that old crow away at last," he said.

CAUGHT NAPPING

It was several days before Mr. Crow stopped sulking. He was very angry with Farmer Green for placing the giant in the cornfield. And he told his friends that he had about made up his mind he would move to some other neighborhood.

"Farmer Green will be sorry after I'm gone," he remarked. "He'll miss me when he finds that his crops are being eaten by mildreds of insects." Whether he meant millions or hundreds it would be hard to say. You see, Mr. Crow was not good at arithmetic. He always had trouble counting higher than ten.

And then, the very day before he had planned to move, Mr. Crow noticed something that made him change his mind. He was sitting in the top of a tall pine, looking mournfully across the cornfield, where he dared not go, when he saw a small bird drop down upon the giant's head and disappear.

"He's eaten her!" Mr. Crow exclaimed. But as he stared, the little bird appeared again and flew away.

Old Mr. Crow knew it was a mother wren; and he was not long in discovering that she had built a nest under the tin pan that the giant wore in place of a hat!

That was enough for Mr. Crow. The secret was out! The thing he had feared was nothing worse than a straw scarecrow, with a stick stuck over its shoulder to look like a gun.

The old gentleman felt quite foolish for a time. But he did not let that fact prevent his scratching up enough corn to make up for the meals he had lost.

After that he quickly recovered his spirits. And he forgot all about moving.

But if Mr. Crow felt merry, you may be sure that Farmer Green did not.

It was his turn to feel foolish. And he vowed that he would get even with

Mr. Crow, if it took him all summer.

Meanwhile, Mr. Crow grew careless. He really thought that Farmer Green wouldn't be able to think of any other way of keeping him out of the cornfield. And he spent so much of his time there that he grew quite fat. He became somewhat short-breathed, too. And his voice grew wheezier than ever. But Mr. Crow did not mind those things. He was getting all the corn he could eat. And he was happy.

Then there came a morning at last, as he soared down upon the cornfield, when he noticed that the huge scarecrow was gone. There was another — a shorter — figure in its place. But to careless Mr. Crow's glance it seemed no different from the scarecrows he had known all his life. He paid little or no attention to the image. It wore the big pan upon its head — he observed that much. And it made him laugh.

Then Mr. Crow began to scratch for his breakfast. But he had not eaten a single kernel when a terrible roar broke the early morning stillness. And there was a sound as of hail falling all around him.

Mr. Crow knew right away what had happened. The scarecrow had come to life and tried to shoot him! And if ever a bird hurried away from that field, it was old Mr. Crow.

It was almost night before he remembered that he had had nothing to eat all day. And so anybody can see how frightened he was....

Farmer Green walked home to his own breakfast with his gun resting upon his shoulder.

"I didn't get him," he told Johnnie. "But I must have scared him out of a year's growth."

V

A GREAT DISAPPOINTMENT

After Farmer Green came so near shooting him, Mr. Crow lost his taste for corn for a whole year. He was afraid it would never come back to him. And he worried so much that he grew quite thin and his feathers began to look rusty. His friends were somewhat alarmed about his health, many of them saying that if they were in Mr. Crow's place they would be careful.

Now, strange as it may seem, that was exactly Mr. Crow's trouble. He was too careful! He was always on the lookout for a gun, or a trap. And being constantly on guard was bad for his nerves.

Luckily, a winter spent in the South did a great deal to improve Mr.

Crow's health, as well as his state of mind. When he came back to

Pleasant Valley the following March he told his cousin Jasper Jay

that he really felt he would be able to eat corn again.

As the spring lengthened, that feeling grew upon Mr. Crow. And when planting-time arrived the black rascal had his old look again.

It was a very solemn look—unless you regarded him closely. But it was a very sly, knowing look if you took the pains to stare boldly into his eye.

Farmer Green would have liked to do that, because then he might have caught old Mr. Crow. As it happened, he did catch sight of Mr. Crow the very first day he began to plant his corn.

"I declare—there's that old crow again!" he exclaimed. "He's come back to bother me once more. But maybe I'm smarter than he thinks!"

Mr. Crow knew better than to come too near the men who were working in the cornfield. He just sat on the fence on the further side of the road and watched them for a while. And he was getting hungrier every minute. But he had no chance to scratch up any corn that day.

11

The next day, however, the men had moved further down the field. Mr. Crow had been waiting for that. He flew to the edge of the ploughed ground, which they had planted the afternoon before, and dug up a kernel of corn.

He didn't stop to look at it. He knew it was corn—just by the feeling of it. And it was inside his mouth in a twinkling.

And in another twinkling it was outside again—for Mr. Crow did not like the taste at all.

"That's a bad one!" he remarked. And then he tried another kernel—and another—and another. But they were all like the first one.

Thereupon, Mr. Crow paused and looked at the corn. And he saw at once that there was something wrong. The kernels were gray, instead of a golden yellow. He pecked at one of them and found that the gray coating hid something black and sticky.

That was tar, though Mr. Crow did not know it. And the gray covering was wood-ashes, in which Farmer Green had rolled the corn after dipping it in tar. The tar made the corn taste bad. And the wood-ashes kept it from sticking to one's fingers.

"This is a great disappointment," said Mr. Crow very solemnly. "Of all the mean tricks that Farmer Green has played on me, this is by far the meanest. It would serve him right if I went away and never caught a single grasshopper or cutworm all summer."

But there were two reasons that prevented Mr. Crow's leaving Pleasant Valley. He liked his old home. And he liked grasshoppers and cutworms, too. So he stayed until October. And the strange part of it was that he never once discovered that Farmer Green had planted tarred corn only in a border around the field. Inside that border the corn was of the good, old yellow kind that Mr. Crow liked.

And so, for once, Farmer Green out-witted old Mr. Crow.

By the end of the summer his corn had grown so tall and borne so many big ears that Farmer Green took some of it to the county fair. And everybody who saw it there said that it was the finest corn that ever was seen in those parts.

VI

MR. CROW IN TROUBLE

After Mr. Crow found that Farmer Green had put tar on his corn, Mr. Crow was so angry that he flew for a good many miles before stopping. And then, as he started to walk along the limb that lead to his house in the tall elm, he noticed for the first time that he could hardly move his right foot.

He looked down and he was startled when he saw that his foot was many times its usual size. Moreover, it did not look like a foot at all, being a strange, huge, shapeless thing.

Old Mr. Crow was alarmed. Never in all his life had he found himself in such a plight. He stayed at home only long enough to tie his foot up in a bandage, which made it look bigger than ever. And then he hurried off as fast as he could fly to call upon Aunt Polly Woodchuck, who was said to be an excellent doctor.

Aunt Polly was at home. And since Mr. Crow could not crawl inside her house, she received him in her dooryard.

As soon as she looked at Mr. Crow's foot Aunt Polly Woodchuck threw up both her hands.

"You have gout!" she cried. "And it's the worst case I ever saw."

That made Mr. Crow feel proud and happy.

"What about a cure?" he inquired. "I shouldn't like to have my foot like this always. If you could cure it in a week I would be satisfied. But I want at least a week in which to show my foot to my friends."

"You'll be lucky if you're better in a month," said Aunt Polly Woodchuck. "You must be very careful about what you eat. You may have all the ginseng and Jimson weed and elecampane that you wish. And drink plenty of catnip tea! But until you're quite well again, don't touch corn, grasshoppers, birds' eggs, field-mice, or elderberries. If you eat such things your other foot may swell. And then you'd be unable to walk at all."

Mr. Crow was no longer happy.

"Those are the things I like best—the last that you mentioned," he said. "And the food you tell me I may have is exactly the kind I've never cared for in the least. As for catnip tea, I can't swallow it!" he groaned.

"Haven't you some other remedy? Can't you give me a pill?"

But Aunt Polly Woodchuck said there was no other way.

"I never can remember what you've told me," Mr. Crow objected.

"I can fix that," said Aunt Polly. And then she went into her house, returning presently with a basket. From the basket she drew forth a handful of herbs, which she gave to Mr. Crow.

"Take these," she said, "and put them in your right-hand pocket. These are what you may eat—a sample of each herb."

Straightway she gave Mr. Crow two more handfuls of food.

"And here," she continued, "here are things you mustn't eat. Put them in your left-hand pocket. And at dinner time to-night you won't have the least bit of trouble knowing what you're allowed to have."

Mr. Crow thanked her politely. But he felt somewhat angry, just the same. He saw that he was going to have a very unpleasant time. For if there was one thing that Mr. Crow liked, it was good food—and plenty of it.

VII

MR. CROW'S BAD MEMORY

It was true, as Mr. Crow had said, that he had a bad memory. By the time he reached home he had forgotten almost everything the famous doctor, Aunt Polly Woodchuck, had said to him. About all Mr. Crow could recall of their talk was that Aunt Polly had told him his swollen foot was caused by gout; and that she had given him samples of such food as he might eat, and also such as he mightn't.

He had put the two kinds in different pockets, just as Aunt Polly had suggested. And all he had to do when he was hungry was to look into his pockets and see what food he might safely choose for his meal. Well, Mr. Crow was hungry as a bear by the time he reached his house. And the first thing he did was to feel in his left-hand pocket. He drew forth a kernel of corn.

"Good!" he cried. "That's exactly what I'd like for my dinner. And if Farmer Green hadn't tarred his corn before planting it I know exactly where I'd go." Then he thought deeply for a few minutes. "I'll go over to the corn-crib and see if I can't find some corn on the ground!" he exclaimed a little later. While he was thinking he ate the sample of corn, without once noticing what he did.

So Mr. Crow flew swiftly to the farm-yard. It happened that there was nobody about. And, luckily, Mr. Crow found enough corn scattered near the door of the corn-crib to furnish him with a good dinner.

The next morning, as soon as it began to grow light (for Mr. Crow was an early riser), he felt in his left-hand pocket once more. And he pulled out an elderberry.

"That won't do!" he said. "It's too early in the season for elderberries." But he ate the sample—though he found it rather dry, for it was a last year's berry. And then he fished a bird's egg out of the same pocket. "My favorite breakfast!" he remarked. He ate the egg. And at once he started out to hunt for more. Some people say that he robbed the nests of several small birds before he had breakfast enough.

Mr. Crow then proceeded to pass the morning very pleasantly, by making calls on his friends. He enjoyed their surprise at seeing his bandaged foot.

"I've the worst case of gout Aunt Polly Woodchuck has ever seen," he told every one with an air of pride.

When lunch time came, it found Mr. Crow with a hearty appetite. And once more he felt in his left-hand pocket to see what he might have for his meal.

He pulled out a squirming field-mouse. Mr. Crow was about to eat him; but the mouse slipped away and hid in a hollow stump. So Mr. Crow lost him. Then he went soaring off across the pasture. And when he came home again he didn't seem hungry at all. Whatever he may have found to eat, it seemed to satisfy him.

By this time Mr. Crow had quite recovered from the fear that had seized him when he first discovered his swollen foot. And before he went to sleep that night he thought he would take the bandage off his foot and look at it. He had some trouble in removing the bandage. And when he had succeeded in unwinding it he could hardly believe his eyes. His foot was its natural size again!

Old Mr. Crow looked at the bandage. And he saw, clinging to it, a mass of caked mud. He could not understand that.

"Anyhow, I'm cured," he said sadly. He was disappointed, because there were still a good many of his friends to whom he had not yet shown his bandaged foot. "I don't consider that Aunt Polly Woodchuck is as good a doctor as people say," Mr. Crow grumbled. "Here she's gone and cured my foot almost a week before I wanted her to!"

And the next day he went over to see the old lady and complain about her mistake.

"What have you been eating?" she asked Mr. Crow.

He told her.

"Ah!" said Aunt Polly. "It's your mistake—and not mine. You ate what was in your left-hand pocket, instead of what was in the right-hand one. If you had followed my instructions everything would have been all right."

Old Mr. Crow felt very much ashamed. There was nothing he could say. So he slunk away and moped for three days.

Though he did not know it, the trouble with his foot was simply this: He had daubed so much tar on his foot, in Farmer Green's cornfield, that the soft earth had stuck to it in a big ball.

Mr. Crow recovered his spirits at last. And neither he nor Aunt Polly Woodchuck ever discovered that he never had gout at all. He forgave her, at last, for having cured his foot too quickly, for the affair gave him something to talk about for a long time afterward. He never tired of telling his friends about the trouble he had had.

But many of the feathered folk in Pleasant Valley grew very weary of the tale before they heard the last of it.

VIII

THE NEW UMBRELLA

Old Mr. Crow was feeling very happy, because he had a new umbrella —
the only umbrella that was owned for miles around. And wherever Mr.
Crow went, the umbrella went too, tucked snugly under his wing.

There was only one thing that could have made Mr. Crow feel any happier;
and that was rain. As soon as it rained he intended to spread the umbrella
over his head and go to call upon all of his friends.

But not a drop of rain had fallen for weeks. And so far as old Mr. Crow
could judge, there wasn't a single sign of a storm anywhere. Nevertheless,
he continued to carry his umbrella every time he stirred away from his
house. And although the weather was so dry, he found a good deal of
pleasure in showing his umbrella to his neighbors.

Now, old Mr. Crow had a cousin of whom you have heard. His name was
Jasper Jay; and he was a great dandy. He always took pride in his
handsome blue suit, of which he was very vain.

Being an inquisitive fellow, Jasper Jay was much interested in Mr. Crow's
umbrella. Whenever he met Mr. Crow he asked the old gentleman to
spread the umbrella; and once Mr. Crow had let Jasper hold it for as long
as ten seconds, "just to see how it felt."

After that Jasper Jay could not get the umbrella out of his mind. He began
calling at Mr. Crow's house every day; and all the time he was there he
never took his eyes off the umbrella.

At last the two cousins met in the woods one day. As usual, Mr. Crow had
his umbrella tucked under his wing. But when Jasper asked him to spread
it, Mr. Crow refused.

"I can't keep putting my umbrella up and down," he said. "If I did, the first
thing I knew it would be worn out; and then what would happen to me if it
should rain?"

"You'd get wet," said Jasper Jay.

"Exactly!" Mr. Crow replied. "And at my age I might take cold and be very ill, perhaps."

"Where are you going?" Jasper inquired pleasantly. He was disappointed; but he did not let his cousin see that.

"I'm on my way to a big meeting of the Crow family," the old gentleman replied.

"And you're taking your umbrella?" Jasper asked, as if he were greatly astonished.

"Why—yes!" Mr. Crow answered. "You seem surprised."

"I am," said Jasper Jay with a sad shake of his head. "I'd hate to risk it, if I were you. There'll be some rough young fellows there and you're likely to lose your umbrella. I'm afraid they'll take it away from you."

Old Mr. Crow looked worried.

"I don't know what to do," he said anxiously. "It's an important meeting. They're expecting me. And I'm late, as it is. If I go back home and leave my umbrella I'm afraid they'll think I'm not coming."

"I suppose I could help you just this once," Jasper Jay remarked. "Of course, it's not a thing I'd do for everybody. But since you're my cousin, if you want me to do it I'll take care of your umbrella until you come back again."

"Will you wait right here?" Mr. Crow asked him.

"Yes!"

"Will you promise not to spread the umbrella?"

At that question Jasper Jay's face fell. But pretty soon he said cheerfully:

"I promise not to put it up—unless it should rain."

Mr. Crow looked carefully at the sky. There was not a cloud to be seen. So he turned to Jasper Jay with a smile and placed the umbrella carefully in his hands.

Then Mr. Crow flew away.

"It certainly can't rain," he said to himself.

Mr. Crow arrived at the meeting quite out of breath. And his friends noticed that he seemed uneasy about something. He kept looking up at the sky and asking everybody what he thought about the weather.

IX

CAUGHT IN THE RAIN

Left alone in the woods with Mr. Crow's umbrella, Jasper Jay had a fine time. First he looked at the umbrella very closely, from the handle to the slender tip. Then he placed it under his wing and strutted back and forth upon the ground, just as he had seen Mr. Crow parade before his friends. And Jasper wished that someone would come along and see him.

But nobody came. So after a while he grew tired of wishing. And the next thing he did was to unfasten the strap that kept the folds of the umbrella wrapped about its stick.

"I'm not putting it up," he told himself. "I didn't promise I wouldn't do this. I only agreed not to spread the umbrella unless it rained."

Just then a low rumble caught his ear.

"That's thunder!" he cried. "I do hope it will rain!"

In a short time the sky grew dark. And pretty soon great drops came pattering down upon the leaves over Jasper's head.

"Hurrah!" he shouted. And then he flew straight up to the very top of a tall tree, where he perched himself on a limb and spread Mr. Crow's umbrella.

Though it was soon raining hard, the rain did not fall any too heavily to please Jasper Jay. He enjoyed the pleasant-sounding patter over his head. And he liked to watch the trickle of the water as it ran off the umbrella and fell upon the leaves beneath him.

Now, while Jasper Jay was having a good time, there was one person who was not enjoying the shower at all—and that was old Mr. Crow. You remember that he had gone to a crows' meeting. And as soon as it began to sprinkle the meeting broke up. Old Mr. Crow was the first one to leave; and he was in a great hurry. He wished he had not left his umbrella with Jasper Jay, for he did not want anybody but himself to use it—especially

22

for the first time. As you know, ever since Mr. Crow had owned his umbrella it had not rained once.

That was why the old gentleman flew away without even stopping to bid his friends good-by. He flew as fast as he could, through the pelting rain. And he had just come in sight of the woods where Jasper had promised to wait for him when the rain suddenly stopped.

As Mr. Crow dropped downward he saw something in a tree-top that made him very angry. It was his umbrella, wide open. And beneath it—though Mr. Crow could not see him—was Jasper Jay.

He was trembling with rage—was Mr. Crow—as he alighted on a limb near his cousin.

"Here, you!" the old gentleman cried. "Put down my umbrella! It's not raining. How dare you sit there with my umbrella spread over your head?"

Jasper Jay closed the umbrella quickly and handed it to Mr. Crow with a smile.

"That's a good umbrella," he remarked. "As you see, I'm not even damp.

But you—ha! ha!—you seem to have been caught out in a heavy shower."

Mr. Crow was dripping. His tail feathers looked quite bedraggled. And he was shaking the drops off his wings.

"It will never happen again," Mr. Crow said hoarsely. "Never again will I go anywhere, rain or shine, without my umbrella. At my age it's very dangerous to get so wet."

"I'd advise you to run through the woods, and then run back again, until you get warm," Jasper Jay suggested. "And since you're my cousin, if you want me to do it I'll help you—and hold your umbrella for you until you return."

But Mr. Crow shook his head.

"I've had enough of your advice," he said sourly. "It might rain again; and then I'd be worse off than ever."

Jasper Jay pretended to be surprised. And he, too, began to tremble and shake. But it was only because he was laughing silently at his cousin.

X

A QUEER TOADSTOOL

Mr. Crow did exactly as he said he would. After the time he was caught out in the shower and got wet he never went even the shortest distance away from home without his umbrella. And he wouldn't even let anybody take his umbrella, in order to look at it.

"It might rain suddenly," Mr. Crow explained. "I might be soaked before

I knew it—and you know that's very dangerous for one of my age."

It was not many days before there was another thunder-shower. And this time Mr. Crow was ready for it. As soon as he felt the first drops he spread his umbrella and raised it above his head. At last he was very, very happy. For the first time in his life he was going to see what it was like to stay out in the rain without getting wet.

Now, it hadn't rained long before Jasper Jay came hurrying up to Mr. Crow, where he sat on Farmer Green's fence, and crawled under the umbrella close beside the old gentleman.

"You don't mind, I hope?" said Jasper Jay.

"Well—n-no!" said Mr. Crow. "It's a big umbrella, fortunately. But I hope no one else comes along."

The words were hardly out of his bill when Mr. Crow noticed a slim, gray fellow, with a bushy tail, bounding toward them on top of the fence.

It was Frisky Squirrel. And he crept close to Mr. Crow, under the umbrella, saying:

"You don't mind, I hope?"

"N-no!" replied Mr. Crow. With Frisky on one side of him and Jasper Jay on the other Mr. Crow thought that maybe he could keep drier because they were there. But he hoped no one else would pass that way.

Well, some one did. Before Mr. Crow knew what had happened, a voice said—right over his shoulder:

"You don't mind, I hope?"

It was Fatty Coon! And Mr. Crow certainly did mind—though he didn't dare say so. In the first place, Mr. Crow was afraid of Fatty Coon. And in the second place, Fatty was so big that he crowded Mr. Crow almost off the fence.

Old Mr. Crow found it very hard to hold the umbrella straight and cling to the fence-rail at the same time. And something seemed to have made the umbrella very heavy. In spite of all he could do, it would tilt. And Mr. Crow crouched under the edge of it, right where the rain poured off. The water dripped inside his collar and ran down his back until he was soaked through and through.

Pretty soon Mr. Crow began to sneeze. At first he sneezed quite softly. But every time it happened he sneezed harder than the time before. And at last he sneezed so violently that he lost his hold on the fence and went tumbling down to the ground, with the umbrella, Jasper Jay, Fatty Coon and Frisky Squirrel on top of him.

As they fell, a huge, long-legged fellow named Christopher Crane alighted on the fence, on the very spot where they had been sitting, and laughed loudly at them.

"What's the joke?" Mr. Crow asked in an angry voice, as he picked himself up. "I don't see anything to laugh at."

"Joke?" said Christopher Crane. "The joke's on me. I thought that thing you have in your hand was a new kind of toadstool, growing on the fence. And here I've been sitting on it all this time and never knew you chaps were under it!"

At that, everybody except Mr. Crow began to laugh, too. But Mr. Crow coughed; and his voice was hoarser than, ever as he said to Christopher Crane:

"I'm wet as I can be. And I've caught a terrible cold. You're a water-bird; and you don't mind a wetting. But for one of my age it's very dangerous."

Then he started homeward. Though it was still raining, he tucked his umbrella under his wing, for he was afraid those rude fellows would crowd under it again.

And before he had reached his house Mr. Crow had made up his mind about something.

XI

MR. CROW'S PLAN

Yes! Old Mr. Crow had made up his mind about something. After Jasper Jay and Frisky Squirrel and Fatty Coon had come and crouched under his umbrella, and Christopher Crane had perched himself on top of it, and Mr. Crow had fallen off the fence, the old gentleman decided that he would take no more chances. The next time it rained he knew exactly what he was going to do.

He said nothing to anyone about his plan. It was a good one—Mr. Crow was sure of that. And he could hardly wait for the next shower, he was so eager to give his scheme a trial. He hoped that there would be a big storm—not merely a quick shower, which would be over before he had had time to enjoy it.

At last the storm came. And for once Mr. Crow was not disappointed. It was the sort of storm that is worth waiting for. The wind had blown hard all day. And the sky had grown almost as black as night. And old Mr. Crow was watching in his house, with his umbrella grasped tight in his hands, waiting for the rain.

When the rain began, it did not fall in a gentle patter. It came with a rush and a roar, driven in white sheets before a mighty wind.

"This is great!" Mr. Crow cried aloud, as he stepped upon a limb outside his house and spread his umbrella.

Now, this is what he had decided to do: He had determined that the very next time it rained he would take his umbrella and fly up into the sky, where he would not be annoyed by anybody coming along to share his shelter with him.

For a moment Mr. Crow balanced himself on the limb. And the next moment, he had jumped. Afterward, he could never remember exactly how it all happened. Everything seemed like a bad dream to old Mr. Crow—such as he sometimes had after eating too heartily of corn.

He felt himself swept up into the sky faster than he had flown for years. He was pitched and tossed about; and in no time at all he was drenched with water—for the cold rain pelted him as much as it pleased. He could only cling to the handle of his umbrella. And so he sailed away, swaying this way and that as the wind caught him, and always climbing higher and higher into the sky.

He passed the top of Blue Mountain almost before he knew it. Looking down, he could see Mrs. Eagle on her nest; and she seemed to be in a flutter of excitement, too. She was frightened; and it was no wonder. For she thought the umbrella was a monstrous bird, coming to snatch her children away from her.

In a few minutes more Mr. Crow had crossed another mountain. He was sailing away from home like a kite that has broken its string. And he was rising so high in the air that he was beginning to grow uneasy. He began to wonder what he had better do.

Of course, there was one thing he didn't have to worry about—and that was falling. But he did want to go home.

You might suppose that he would have done that long before. But the trouble was, he didn't want to lose his umbrella. He thought a great deal of it; and he didn't know where he could get another. (You must not forget that it was the only umbrella in Pleasant Valley.)

Old Mr. Crow had a hard time deciding just what to do. First, he thought he would let go of the umbrella. Then he thought he wouldn't. Next, he thought he would. And after that he thought he wouldn't, again.

Perhaps he would still be changing his mind like that if something hadn't happened. Anyhow, all at once the umbrella turned inside out. And Mr. Crow began to fall.

But he didn't fall far. For as soon as he realized what was going on he let go of his umbrella-handle, spread his wings, and soared down to the ground.

He made no attempt to find his way home until the next day, but spent the night in an evergreen grove. And he didn't feel as badly about losing his umbrella as you would have thought, for he said that ever since he had owned it he had caught a wetting when it rained. And since that was the case, he was better off without an umbrella, anyhow.

A RACE WITH THE TRAIN

Old Mr. Crow was fond of gay clothes. Perhaps it was because he was so black that he always chose bright colors. Anyhow, so long as he could wear a bright red coat and a yellow necktie—or a bright red necktie and a yellow coat—he was generally quite happy.

All his neighbors knew who he was as far as they could see him. No matter if they caught only a flash of yellow or of red, they were pretty safe in saying, "There goes old Mr. Crow!"

Well, it happened that during the summers that he spent in Pleasant

Valley Mr. Crow sometimes went on excursions.

"It's so dull here!" he would often say. "I like to see things happen, once in a while." And that was the reason why he was often to be seen flying far down to the other end of the valley, over the village. There were many interesting sights there.

What Mr. Crow liked most of all was to watch the trains puffing along the railroad, which ran close to the river in that part of Pleasant Valley.

Sometimes he flew directly over the trains and raced with them. He often claimed that they were always trying to beat him. "But they can't do it," he boasted.

At last there came a day when something happened that made Mr. Crow feel prouder than ever. He had gone down to the village, wearing his bright red coat. And a little way beyond the furthest house he perched in a tree by the side of the railroad and waited for the train to pass. He had heard it snorting at the station and he knew it was about to start.

Pretty soon the train came thundering up the track. And as soon as it reached him Mr. Crow started to race with it. He had no trouble in beating it, as he always did. And then he did something he had never done before.

As soon as he had passed the engine he swooped down and flew right across the track in front of it.

All at once the train set up a terrible noise. It seemed to Mr. Crow that it ground its teeth. And it came to a sudden stop, hissing as if it were very angry.

Old Mr. Crow was the least bit startled. He alighted in the top of a tall elm. And while he watched, two men jumped down from the engine and walked along the track for a while.

Then they crawled back into the engine; and the train went slowly on again.

"That's queer!" said Mr. Crow to himself. "I never saw that happen before. It looks to me as if the train was pretty angry because I beat it. And if that's the case, I'm coming back here to-morrow at the same hour and race the train again."

You can see just from that that Mr. Crow was something of a tease. All his life he had teased his neighbors. And now he felt more important than ever, because he thought he had found a way to tease a railroad train.

XIII

THE GAME OF CHECKERS

Mr. Crow told all his neighbors that he had made the train angry with him. And he invited everyone to come down to the village with him the following day, to enjoy the sport.

"I'm going to race the train again," Mr. Crow explained. "And I shall fly right in front of it, too—just as I did to-day. You'll see what a fuss it will make. And if you don't say it's a good joke, I'll never wear a checkered red coat again."

The next day Jasper Jay invited Mr. Crow to take part in a game of checkers. Whenever anybody in the neighborhood wanted to play checkers, he had to ask Mr. Crow, on account of having to use his checkered red coat for the board.

Mr. Crow accepted the invitation.

"But I shall have to stop at exactly sixteen minutes past two," he said. "The train starts from the village at half past two sharp; and I don't want to be late."

"Very well!" Jasper Jay agreed. "I shall want to stop then myself, because I'm coming along with you to see the fun."

They had played twenty-seven games of checkers. And they were in the midst of the twenty-eighth when Mr. Crow suddenly cocked his eye at the sun.

"Goodness!" he exclaimed, springing up quickly. "It's fifteen and a half minutes after two; and I shall have to be starting for the village." He reached for his checkered red coat, which was spread upon the ground between them.

"Wait a moment!" Jasper Jay cried. "I'd suggest your leaving your coat right where it is. Then we can come back to our game after we've had our fun with the train. I'm going to win the game, so it's hardly fair not to finish it."

Now, Mr. Crow had not liked the idea of leaving his handsome red coat upon the ground. But he never could bear the thought of being beaten. And Jasper Jay's remark made him feel quite peevish.

"I fully expect to win this game myself," the old gentleman said somewhat stiffly. "So I'll leave my coat here as you suggest. But I shall have to go this instant, for I must stop at my house and get my yellow coat. Of course I can't go down to the village in my shirtsleeves."

He hurried away then, with Jasper Jay close behind him. And as soon as Mr. Crow had put on his bright yellow coat the two checker-players started for the village.

When Jasper and Mr. Crow reached the tree where the old gentleman had waited for the train the day before, they found as many as a dozen of their neighbors already there. Even as Mr. Crow dropped down upon a limb, he could hear the train coming up the track.

Mr. Crow's friends in the tree chose the best seats they could find, in order to get a good view of the race. And at the foot of the tree Jimmy Rabbit stood on tiptoe. He had often wished he could climb a tree—but never so much as then.

XIV

THE LUCKY LAUGH

As the train drew nearer to the tree where Mr. Crow and his friends were waiting, it gave a loud shriek.

"You hear that?" said Mr. Crow. "It's still angry." And he shouted an impudent caw-caw in reply.

In a moment more the race began. Mr. Crow had no trouble in beating the train, just as he always had. And when he had passed it he dropped quickly and swerved across the track ahead of it.

To his great surprise the train never faltered. It kept straight on, going faster and faster. And the first thing Mr. Crow knew, the last car had whipped around a curve and passed out of sight.

Poor Mr. Crow felt very downcast. He would have liked to hurry home at once, because he hated to face his friends. But he knew they would follow him if he flew away. So he went back to meet them, wearing a bold smile.

"Did you see what happened?" he inquired. "The train was afraid to stop!"

Everybody laughed when Mr. Crow said that. People knew him too well to be deceived by him.

"I suppose your yellow coat frightened it," Jasper Jay jeered. "It's too bad you didn't wear your checkered red one."

At that remark Jimmy Rabbit pricked up his long ears.

"Did you wear your red coat yesterday?" he asked Mr. Crow.

"Yes!" Mr. Crow replied gruffly. He did not like being questioned by a mere youngster like Jimmy Rabbit.

"And you say the train stopped when you flew in front of it yesterday?"

Mr. Crow grunted. But Jimmy Rabbit knew that he meant "Yes!"

"That's it!" Jimmy Rabbit cried. And he jumped up and down in his excitement.

"That's what?" asked Mr. Crow in a sulky tone.

"I'll tell you!" said Jimmy. "Yesterday the train stopped because it saw your red coat. That's the way to stop a train. You wave a red flag or a red lantern at a train and it will always stop. But I've noticed that a train pays no attention to any other color. Now, you could wave something green, or yellow, or blue in front of a train; and no matter how hard you waved, it would go right on as if it never saw you at all."

"Maybe you know," Mr. Crow snapped. "And maybe you don't. I said the train was afraid to stop. And I still think so."

Jimmy Rabbit winked at the crowd in the tree.

"I must hop along now," he told them. "I'm glad I came to see the race, for it has been even more fun than I expected."

Then Jasper Jay gave Mr. Crow a great start.

"It's too bad—" he said—"it's too bad you can't wear your red coat any more, Mr. Crow."

"How's that?" asked Mr. Crow quickly.

"You promised that if we didn't say it was a good joke you'd never wear a checkered red coat again."

Now, Mr. Crow had forgotten all about that remark. And for a moment he looked worried. Then he turned cheerful all at once.

"Look here!" he cried. "When I came back to this tree you all laughed, didn't you?"

Everybody admitted that.

"Then there must have been a good joke somewhere," Mr. Crow said. "And I shall wear my red coat as often as I please."

No one really cared, anyhow, whether he did or whether he didn't. But Mr. Crow was angry with Jasper Jay. And he refused to finish the game of checkers with him.

XV

MR. CROW'S NEW COAT

When Mr. Crow decided, one fall, that he would stay in Pleasant Valley during the winter, instead of going South, he remembered at once that he would need a thick overcoat.

That was when he went to Mr. Frog's tailor's shop, for Mr. Frog, you know, was a tailor.

"I want you to make me a warm overcoat." Mr. Crow told him. "Can you do it?"

"Certainly!" said Mr. Frog. "You've come to the right place. Everybody says that I'm the best tailor in Pleasant Valley." And that was quite true—because he was the only one. "What'll you have—stripes, checks, or spots?" Mr. Frog asked briskly.

"What do you suggest?" Mr. Crow replied. He had not thought much about his new coat—except that he wanted it to be warm.

"Spots, by all means!" said Mr. Frog. "I always wear 'em myself. They're the best, to my mind. For if you happen to get a spot on your coat, what's one spot more?"

"That's a good idea," Mr. Crow said. "And how much will you ask to make me a spotted coat?"

"I charge by the spot," said Mr. Frog. "The more spots, the more the coat will cost. So I'd advise you to take a coat with large spots, because there'll be fewer of 'em and the price will be less."

"That's a good idea, too," said old Mr. Crow. "You may make my coat of this!" He pointed to a piece of blue cloth with yellow spots about the size of a dollar and a quarter.

"Good!" said Mr. Frog. Then he measured Mr. Crow. And then he measured the cloth. And then he scratched some figures on a flat stone.

37

"There'll be thirteen spots on your coat and that'll make just thirteen that you'll owe me."

"Thirteen what?" asked Mr. Crow.

"Ah! That's the question!" said Mr. Frog, mysteriously. "I'll tell you when your coat's finished. And you can pay me then. It's what is known as 'spot cash,'" he added.

"Very well!" Mr. Crow answered. "And I'll come back—"

"To-morrow!" said the tailor.

When to-morrow came, Mr. Crow flew over to the pond where Mr. Frog had his tailor's shop. And that spry gentleman slipped Mr. Crow's new coat upon him. While Mr. Crow stood stiffly in the middle of the floor Mr. Frog pulled the coat here and patted it there. He backed away and looked at it, with his head on one side; and then he stood on his head and looked at it, with his legs dangling in the air.

"It's a perfect fit," he assured Mr. Crow, finally. And then he caught up a needle and thread and busied himself behind Mr. Crow's back for a long time.

"What are you doing?" Mr. Crow inquired at last. "I'm getting tired of standing still."

"Just fixing it!" answered Mr. Frog. "It'll be finished in a minute."

And it was. He stuck his needle into Mr. Crow, to let him know it was done.

Mr. Crow jumped half way across the room. "Why did you do that?" he asked hotly.

"I wanted to break my thread," Mr. Frog explained pleasantly. "It's the quickest way of breaking a thread that I know of."

"You look out, or I'll break something else for you," Mr. Crow squawked, for he was thoroughly enraged. "And now," he added, "I'll pay you what I owe before leaving. I owe thirteen of something."

Then Mr. Frog surprised him.

"I've decided not to take any pay," he announced. "I hear that thirteen is an unlucky number."

"Is that so?" Mr. Frog exclaimed. "Perhaps it is. If you had stuck your needle into me thirteen times it certainly would have been unlucky for you."

On the whole Mr. Crow was well pleased with his bargain. He was glad that he had asked Mr. Frog to make a coat for him. Indeed, if only the tailor had not stabbed him with his needle, he would have returned to the shop at once and ordered Mr. Frog to make him a pair of trousers — with thirteen spots on them.

XVI

A TIGHT FIT

Now, a certain thing happened that made Mr. Crow change his mind about staying North for the winter. It had something to do with nuts, and Frisky Squirrel, and Sandy Chipmunk. But that is another story; and you may already have heard it.

Anyhow, Mr. Crow suddenly decided that he would have to fly southward, after all. He was disappointed, because he didn't like the thought of having to make so long a journey. Moreover, he had his new blue coat with the yellow spots, which Mr. Frog had made for him. It was a handsome coat. And everybody said it was very becoming to Mr. Crow. But he knew it was altogether too warm to wear to his home in the South where the weather was sure to be mild.

"I'll have to leave my new coat behind," he said to himself in a sad voice. "It's almost too heavy to wear even here, though it is fall. I hate to do it; but I'd better take it off and hide it somewhere. There might be some cold days next spring when I'd be glad of a thick, warm coat."

So the old gentleman started to unbutton his new coat, which he had worn all day, ever since Mr. Frog had slipped it on him early in the morning. Anyone might think that it would have been an easy matter to unbutton the coat, for Mr. Frog had sewed a double row of big brown buttons down the front of it. But for some time Mr. Crow fumbled with one of them in vain.

"Ha!" he exclaimed at last. "This is stupid of me! I'm trying to unbutton the wrong row of buttons." Then he fumbled with one of the buttons of the other row. But strange to say, he was no more successful than before. He struggled with all the buttons in that row (there were five of them). And then he tried the other five, one after another.

Mr. Crow couldn't understand it. He wanted more than ever to take the coat off, because his efforts to unbutton it had made him quite warm.

40

"I shall have get somebody to help me," he said at last. "It may be that my eyesight is failing — though I haven't noticed before that there was anything the matter with it.... There's my cousin, Jasper Jay! I'll ask him to unbutton my coat." And he called to Jasper, who had just alighted on a stump not far away.

To Mr. Crow's dismay, his cousin refused to assist him.

"I know you too well," said Jasper Jay. "You want to play some trick on me. If the buttons were on the back of your coat I might help you. But they're right in front of you; and they're so big that a blind person couldn't help finding them, even on the darkest night.... No! You can't fool me this time!"

"Very well!" Mr. Crow croaked. "If you won't help me, there are plenty of other people who'll be glad to." And he flew away in something very like a temper.

To Mr. Crow's surprise he couldn't find anyone that would unbutton his new coat for him; like Jasper Jay, everybody was afraid that Mr. Crow meant to play a trick on him.

Mr. Crow was beginning to be frightened. He had called on all his friends in Pleasant Valley except one. And if that one should refuse, Mr. Crow didn't know what he could do. He had liked his spotted coat. But now he began to hate it. And he wanted to slip out of it and never see it again.

So Mr. Crow hurried over to the swamp where Fatty Coon lived.

XVII

THE STRANGE BUTTONS

To Mr. Crow's delight, it did not occur to Fatty Coon that Mr. Crow might be playing a trick on him. You see, as was usually the case, Fatty was hungry. And he had no thought for anything except food. When Mr. Crow explained what a fix he was in, and asked Fatty to unbutton his coat for him, Fatty stepped up to him at once.

But he didn't try to unbutton the coat. He sniffed at the buttons, while his face wore a puzzled look. And then he began to smile.

"I'll tell you what I'll do!" Fatty said. "If you'll give me these buttons, I'll take them off for you. And then, of course, you'll have no more trouble with your coat. You can throw it off any time you please."

"Good!" Mr. Crow exclaimed. "The buttons shall be yours. I don't want them, for I shall never wear this coat again."

So Fatty Coon set to work to take off the buttons. He removed them in a very odd way, too. Instead of tearing them off he began eating them!

"Goodness!" Mr. Crow cried. "Aren't you afraid you'll be ill?"

But Fatty Coon never answered. He kept on nibbling the buttons and crunching them in his mouth. And he never stopped until he had swallowed the very last one.

Then he smacked his lips (for he knew no better).

"Those were the finest gingersnaps I ever tasted," he remarked. "It's a pity there weren't a baker's dozen of them, instead of only ten."

Old Mr. Crow nearly fell over, he was so surprised. He had never dreamed that those big brown buttons, which Mr. Frog had sewed upon his coat, were nothing but gingersnaps.

"If I'd known that I would have eaten them myself!" he exclaimed. "But I don't care. Now that I can get out of this heavy coat, I'm satisfied."

But to Mr. Crow's dismay, the coat clung round him as tightly as ever. He couldn't throw it open at all. And he turned the least bit pale.

"This is strange!" he murmured. "What can be the matter, I wonder!"

Fatty Coon looked at the coat again. And then he laughed.

"The trouble—" he said—"the trouble is, there are no buttonholes! Your coat doesn't open in front. And it doesn't open anywhere else, either. It's sewed on you, Mr. Crow."

Poor Mr. Crow began to feel faint. He leaned against a tree and did not speak for some time. But he was thinking deeply. And all at once he understood what had happened.

"It's all the fault of that silly tailor, Mr. Frog!" he groaned. "He made me stand still a long time. And that was when he sewed my coat up the back…. What can I do?" he asked helplessly.

"If I were you I'd go straight to Mr. Frog's shop and make him take the stitches out," Fatty Coon said. "And if he has any more of those gingersnaps, I wish you'd let me know."

AN UNLUCKY NUMBER

As soon as old Mr. Crow pushed open the door of Mr. Frog's tailor's shop, Mr. Frog jumped up quickly. He had been sitting cross-legged upon a table, sewing. And when he leaped off the table he sprang so high that his head struck the ceiling.

"What's that noise?" Mr. Crow asked him nervously, when Mr. Frog had landed upon his feet. "It sounded like thunder; but there's not a cloud in the sky."

"It was my head," Mr. Frog explained. "It hit the ceiling, you know."

"Oh!" said Mr. Crow. "It made a very hollow sound. But I am not surprised. I have already learned that your head is quite empty."

"It's certainly not solid," Mr. Frog agreed pleasantly. No matter what happened, he never lost his temper.

But Mr. Crow was different. He was angry.

"You've got me into a pretty fix!" said he. "And now you must get me out of it."

"I suppose you want more buttons," Mr. Prog observed. "I noticed as you came in that you had lost every one."

"No!" Mr. Crow told him. "What I want is to get out of this coat. I've decided to spend the winter in the South, after all. And here you've been and gone and sewed the coat on me, and left me no way at all to slip out of it."

"I beg your pardon," the tailor replied politely. "Pardon me—but I think you are mistaken. I left four openings through which anyone could crawl out."

Old Mr. Crow looked puzzled.

"I should like to know where they are," he said.

"The neck, the skirts, and the two sleeves!" Mr. Frog told him.

At that Mr. Crow looked at him severely.

"How could you expect me to slip through any of those places?" he asked.

"Why—" said the tailor—"I thought it would be easy for you. I've always heard you were a very slippery customer."

When he said that, Mr. Crow made some queer noises in his throat, much as if he were choking.

"Are you ill?" the tailor cried.

"Just a frog in my throat!" Mr. Crow answered.

As he said that. Mr. Frog leaped toward the door. He was a jumpy sort of person. When anything startled him you could never tell in what direction he might spring. And he was now about to rush out of his shop when Mr. Crow caught him and dragged him back.

"You can't go," he shouted, "until you've taken the stitches out of the back of my coat."

"Oh, certainly!" Mr. Frog quavered. And he set to work at once to open the back seam of Mr. Crow's coat.

He was a spry worker—was Mr. Frog. In less time than it takes to tell it he had ripped the back of the coat from collar to hem.

And old Mr. Crow was no less spry in pulling the coat off and flinging it into a corner.

"There!" Mr. Crow cried. "There's your coat with the thirteen spots on it! I certainly don't want it, for it has caused me no end of trouble." Then he turned and hurried out of the shop, without stopping even to thank Mr. Frog for what he had done.

Before Mr. Crow was out of hearing, the tailor thrust his head through the doorway and called to the departing Mr. Crow.

"I told you—" said Mr. Frog—"I told you thirteen was an unlucky number."

XIX

THE SHOE-STORE

"Dear me!" old Mr. Crow exclaimed one day. "I see I shall have to get some new shoes. I've had these only about ten years and they're worn through already. The trouble is, I don't know where to buy any more." He was talking to his cousin, Jasper Jay.

"I can tell you," said Jasper. "That Rabbit boy — the one they call Jimmy — has a shoe-store. You know he's always trying something new. He has had a barber's shop; and he's been a tooth-puller. And now he has opened a shoe-store over in the meadow."

"I'm glad to know it," Mr. Crow replied, "though I must say I wish it was somebody else. There's something about that Rabbit boy that I don't like. Maybe it's the way he wags his ears and wriggles his nose. And he's always jumping."

"He's a bright young fellow," said Jasper Jay.

Old Mr. Crow coughed.

"A little too bright, sometimes," he ventured. "But he'll have to be a good deal brighter to play any of his tricks on me."

"You think you're enough for him?" Jasper inquired.

"Think?" cried Mr. Crow. "I know I am. And though I hate to get any shoes in his shop, I'm afraid I shall have to just this once."

Later that day Mr. Crow went to the shoe-shop in the meadow. And Jimmy Rabbit was delighted to see him.

"Come right in!" he invited Mr. Crow. "I see you need some new shoes. And you've made no mistake in coming here for them."

"I hope not," Mr. Crow responded gruffly. He went inside the store and sat down. And Jimmy Rabbit knelt before him and measured one of his feet.

Now, Mr. Crow had enormous feet. Big feet had always run — or walked — in his family. And though he couldn't any more help the size of his feet than the size of his bill, old Mr. Crow was very touchy in respect to them. He grew angry at once.

"What do you mean by measuring my feet?" he croaked. "I didn't come here to be insulted, you know."

Jimmy Rabbit looked up at him mildly.

"I just wanted to find out how small your feet are," he explained politely enough. "Sometimes people come here with feet so small that I can't fit them. And when I looked at yours I was afraid that might be the case."

"Oh!" said Mr. Crow. The answer pleased him. "Show me the best pair of shoes you have," he ordered.

So Jimmy Rabbit began to search his shelves. To tell the truth, he was puzzled. He had no shoes big enough for Mr. Crow. But he did not dare tell the old gentleman that, because he knew Mr. Crow would be very angry.

At last Jimmy Rabbit found the biggest shoes in the place. And he showed them to Mr. Crow, who seemed much pleased.

"I'll try them on," Mr. Crow said.

Jimmy Rabbit held out the shoes, hoping that Mr. Crow would take them.

But Mr. Crow had no such notion in his head.

"I mean, you may try them on me" he added.

"You didn't say that," Jimmy Rabbit reminded him.

"No further remarks are necessary," Mr. Crow screamed in a shrill voice.

And at that Jimmy Rabbit knelt before him once more and began to crowd one of Mr. Crow's feet into one of the shoes.

Jimmy struggled for a long time without saying a word. But Mr. Crow said several words under his breath, for Jimmy was hurting him dreadfully.

There were two reasons for that. In the first place, the shoe was much too small for Mr. Crow. And in the second, Jimmy Rabbit was putting the left shoe on Mr. Crow's right foot.

But neither of them knew that second reason.

XX

OLD SHOES FOR NEW

Old Mr. Crow was too proud to admit that the shoe Jimmy Rabbit was pulling upon his right foot was too small for him. But he would have objected, to be sure, had he known that it was the left shoe. He would have objected likewise when Jimmy crammed his left foot into the right shoe a few minutes later. But Mr. Crow only knew that his feet already ached.

"Now just stand on them!" Jimmy Rabbit said at last.

And Mr. Crow stood up.

"Now walk a bit," the shoe merchant continued.

But Mr. Crow could not walk. He hobbled a short distance. And then he sank down with a groan.

"They don't hurt you, do they?" Jimmy Rabbit asked him.

And Mr. Crow shook his head. He thought he could do that truthfully. What he felt was far worse than a mere hurt. It was torture—that was certainly what it was.

Of course Jimmy Rabbit knew what the trouble was—or part of it, at least. He knew that Mr. Crow's toes were doubled up inside the shoes. And it was on the tip of his tongue to suggest to Mr. Crow that he have his toes cut off. But a better way soon occurred to Jimmy Rabbit.

"I know you'll find these shoes very comfortable—after they're finished," he told Mr. Crow.

"Finished!" Mr. Crow exclaimed. "Do you mean to say they're only partly made?"

"There's just one more thing to do to them," Jimmy Rabbit explained. "The holes haven't been cut in them yet."

"Holes!" said Mr. Crow. "What holes?"

"Why, the holes for your toes, of course!" Jimmy Rabbit answered.

49

"Maybe you didn't know that shoes are to be worn like that this summer.

It makes them much cooler in hot weather."

Well, Mr. Crow liked the idea. He said so, too. He certainly couldn't wear the shoes as they were. And if everybody else was going to wear shoes with toe-holes, he didn't want to be behind the times. But he hadn't seen anybody with shoes made after that fashion. And he told Jimmy Rabbit as much.

"Ah!" said Jimmy Rabbit. "Quite true! You'll be the first in Pleasant Valley, Mr. Crow. You'll set the fashion, instead of following it. Better be first than last, you know!"

Old Mr. Crow agreed to that. So he let Jimmy Rabbit cut as many holes in the shoes as he had toes — that made four holes in each shoe.

And then Mr. Crow thrust his toes through the holes. To his great delight he could walk with ease and comfort. And he was about to leave the store when Jimmy Rabbit stopped him.

"Haven't you forgotten something?" he asked.

"I don't think so," Mr. Crow replied.

"Yes, you have!" Jimmy Rabbit insisted. "You've forgotten your bill!"

Mr. Crow looked at him in amazement. And then he felt of his face.

"None of your tricks, young man!" he cried. "My bill is right where it belongs. How could I forget it, I should like to know?"

"You don't understand," said Jimmy Rabbit. "What I mean is this: You haven't paid me for the shoes."

"Oh!" said Mr. Crow. And he looked away quickly. "Well, you may keep my old shoes. I'm sure that's a fair exchange."

And he pretended to be surprised when Jimmy Rabbit did not agree with him.

"Your old shoes are full of holes," Jimmy objected. "I don't want them."

And there Mr. Crow had him.

"These shoes I have on are full of holes, too," he declared. "And if one hole isn't just as good as another, then I may as well go back to school again." And with that he stalked angrily away.

As it happened, old Mr. Crow had never been to school in his life. But he thought the remark sounded well. And it seemed to keep Jimmy Rabbit quiet. He couldn't think of a thing to say until long after Mr. Crow had gone.

And then it was too late.

XXI

THE CROW CAUCUS

"Where are all those crows going?" Johnnie Green asked his father one evening. He pointed to a long line of big black birds that straggled across the sky. They came from across the valley. And they were travelling fast toward the pine woods near the foot of Blue Mountain. "They seem to be in a hurry," said Johnnie Green.

His father took one look at the procession and laughed.

"They're going to a crow caucus, I guess," he answered.

And then Johnnie wanted to know what a caucus was. He asked so many other questions, too, that Farmer Green didn't succeed in answering them all until they had almost finished their supper.

Now, it was the custom of old Mr. Crow and many of his dusky friends to gather at sunset in the pine woods and hold a meeting. That was what Farmer Green meant when he said they were going to a caucus. And if he could have been there himself he would have been astonished at the things he would have heard.

But for some reason he was never invited to attend one of those twilight meetings. Perhaps it was because disagreeable remarks were sometimes made about Farmer Green!

On that evening when Johnnie noticed the flight of Mr. Crow's cronies toward the woods something happened at the meeting that displeased that old gentleman. Being the biggest—as well as the oldest—crow in the neighborhood, for years past he had called every such meeting to order. And he had always done most of the talking, too.

But old Mr. Crow was late that night. When he reached the pine woods he found that a stranger had taken his accustomed seat in a great tree and was already addressing the gathering in a loud and commanding voice.

And nobody paid any attention to old Mr. Crow. Nobody made room for him. He had to take a back seat on a limb that was crowded with boisterous young fellows, who kept pushing and poking one another. It was most annoying.

"Who's that person that's so fond of hearing himself talk?" Mr. Crow asked someone in the next tree. He spoke in such a loud voice that everybody could hear him. And the stranger cried out sharply:

"Silence!"

Thereupon everyone looked around at Mr. Crow and frowned.

He felt both angry and uncomfortable. And for a little while he sat as still as he could and listened to the stranger's remarks.

Now, the newcomer was talking about the hard times. He said that there weren't as many grasshoppers as usual that year, and that Farmer Green had put tar on his corn before he planted it and that the rats had stolen most of his young chickens (of course that left very few for them), and that the wild berry crop was poor.

Everybody agreed with the stranger. And everybody nodded his head, as if to say, "That's quite true!"—at least, everybody but Mr. Crow. He was determined that he would not agree with anything the stranger said. And so he shouted, "Nonsense!" at the top of his lungs.

A murmur ran through the meeting. And there were cries of "Put him out!"

"That's what I say, too!" Mr. Crow bellowed.

And then he could hardly believe his ears when someone near him said,

"They mean you!"

XXII

THE TEST

Well, it was no wonder that Mr. Crow was surprised when he found that some people wanted to put him out of the meeting just because he had said one word. Had he not always talked more than anybody else at those sunset meetings in the pine woods?

Luckily, no one made a move to oust him. And he managed to keep silent for a little while. But he was so angry that he did not hear what the stranger was saying. At last, however, Mr. Crow began to pay attention again.

"Do you want to know why times are hard and food is scarce in this neighborhood?" the impudent fellow asked.

Everybody except old Mr. Crow answered, "Yes!" And after the echo had died away the stranger continued:

"It's because you need a new leader," he declared. "I understand that a person called 'Old Mr. Crow' has been your leader for a good many years. And my advice to you, friends, is this:Get rid of him!"

A good deal of applause greeted his words. But some of the older and wiser of his listeners shook their heads.

"Who is there that could take Mr. Crow's place?" a voice called.

At that question the stranger coughed slightly and said:

"Of course, I wouldn't suggest any one specially, being a newcomer here myself. And if the position were offered to me, I don't know that I could accept it, though I have had so much experience."

The young fellows on the limb with Mr. Crow at once set up a great cawing.

"We want you!" they chanted. Old Mr. Crow might have been a scarecrow, for all the attention they paid to him. And he did not dare open his mouth. Many others took up the cry. And a great hub-bub arose—a beating of

54

wings, and flying up and down, and jostling. Some of the younger ones squawked like chickens; others pretended to cry like children. But most of the company cawed in their loudest tones, until the whole valley rang with the uproar.

Then one of old Mr. Crow's best friends spoke up and said:

"It's plain that a good many people want you for a leader, stranger."

"Then I'd be very happy to act as such," the bold fellow replied. "And

I'll begin at once."

But the elderly person who had just spoken said that there was no hurry and that the stranger ought first to be put to a test.

"We want to make sure that you're a good leader," he explained. "And I would suggest that you go to see Farmer Green to-morrow, tell him that we object to his putting tar on his corn, and ask him not to do it again next spring."

The stranger looked somewhat uneasy, as he listened. But after he had pondered for a few moments he said briskly:

"I'll do that! I'll go to Farmer Green to-morrow (he won't be busy, for to-morrow's Sunday), and I'll make him agree to what you want."

"We'll meet again on Monday, at sunset," Mr. Crow's friend announced.

And then the meeting broke up in the wildest disorder.

As for old Mr. Crow, he crept away without speaking to anyone. And always, before, he had made more noise than any ten of the others.

XXIII

THE WHITE FLAG

Unhappy Mr. Crow could scarcely eat a mouthful of food after that meeting on Saturday night, when he found the stranger talking to the gathering. He was worried, because he knew that if the stranger succeeded in getting Farmer Green to promise that he would not put tar on his corn the following spring, everybody would choose the newcomer to be the leader of all the crows in Pleasant Valley. And that was an honor that old Mr. Crow had had for years.

For two whole days he sulked at home. He wouldn't even go to his door when anybody knocked. But on Monday evening Mr. Crow was the first to reach the meeting-place in the pine woods, long before sunset. He sat himself down in the leader's seat. And there he intended to stay as long as he could.

At last his neighbors came straggling to the woods. And when the stranger arrived he seemed annoyed because he could not have Mr. Crow's seat. And he said in an undertone to Mr. Crow:

"I advise you to go home."

The old gentleman glared at him. And he answered in a loud voice:

"I advise you to go home yourself — if you have a home to go to!"

Now, some people thought that Mr. Crow's answer was a good one. So they laughed. And that made the stranger feel quite uncomfortable.

But there were others who spoke up and said that Mr. Crow's remark was very unkind. They knew that the stranger had a beautiful home, further north, because he had told them all about it.

And that made him feel better once more.

Then old Mr. Crow called the meeting to order. And immediately the stranger announced in a loud voice:

"I saw Farmer Green and he has surrendered!"

Then there was even more noise than is usual at a crow caucus. It was a long time before old Mr. Crow could quiet the meeting. But he succeeded at last. And when it was still he said to the stranger:

"How do you know Farmer Green has surrendered?"

It was so quiet that you could have heard a pine-needle fall, for everyone was straining his ears to hear.

"Farmer Green hung out the white flag to-day!" the stranger told them.

Well, then there was another outburst. Of course, everybody knew that the white flag was the sign of surrender. And it was some time before old Mr. Crow could restore order.

"I doubt it!" he cried, to everyone's astonishment.

"It's true!" a voice shouted. "I know, for I saw — caw — caw! There was not only one white flag; there were dozens of them!"

And then Mr. Crow surprised them by laughing loudly. He stopped at last and wiped his eyes — for he had actually wept, both with joy and amusement.

"What day is this?" he inquired.

And a hundred voices answered: "Monday!"

"Right!" said Mr. Crow. "And Monday is washday at the farmhouse. Those white flags at Farmer Green's — they were the family wash, hung out on the line to dry!"

Then all Mr. Crow's neighbors crowded around him and told him that they wanted him for their leader — and that they always had. They said that they knew all the time that the stranger was a fraud.

"Where is he?" someone inquired. "Let's fix him!"

But when they turned to look for the stranger they couldn't find him anywhere. He had vanished. Though Mr. Crow and his friends searched far and wide for the bold, bad fellow, their efforts were all in vain. During the bustle that had followed Mr. Crow's short speech the newcomer had quietly made his escape. And no doubt it was just as well for him that he left the meeting when he did.

Some said he had hurried off towards the north; while others claimed that he had gone in a southerly direction. And though they have kept an eye out for him ever since, they have not found — or "fixed him" — yet.